★ THE GREATEST EVENT IN SPORTS HISTORY ★

FLOAT AND STING!

ONE ROUND
WITH
★ MUHAMMAD ★
ALI

STONE ARCH BOOKS
MINNEAPOLIS   SAN DIEGO

FLOAT AND STING!

WRITTEN BY *DAVIS MILLER*

ILLUSTRATED BY *ANDRES ESPARZA*

COLOR BY *JESUS ABURTO*

DESIGNER: *BRANN GARVEY*

ART DIRECTOR: *BOB LENTZ*

EDITOR: *DONALD LEMKE*

CREATIVE DIRECTOR: *HEATHER KINDSETH*

ASSOC. EDITOR: *SEAN TULIEN*

EDITORIAL DIRECTOR: *MICHAEL DAHL*

Graphic Flash is published by Stone Arch Books, 151 Good Counsel Drive, P.O. Box 669, Mankato, Minnesota 56002
www.stonearchbooks.com Copyright © 2009 by Stone Arch Books. All rights reserved. No part of this publication may be
reproduced in whole or in part, or stored in a retrieval system, or transmitted in any form or by any means, electronic,
mechanical, photocopying, recording, or otherwise, without written permission of the publisher.

Library of Congress Cataloging-in-Publication Data
Miller, Davis.
 Float and sting! : one round with Muhammad Ali / by Davis Worth Miller ; illustrated by Andres Esparza.
    p. cm. -- (Graphic flash)
  ISBN 978-1-4342-1578-9 (library binding)
 [1. Physical fitness--Fiction. 2. Self-confidence--Fiction. 3. Boxing--Fiction. 4. Ali, Muhammad, 1942---Fiction.] I.
Esparza, Andres, ill. II. Title.
  PZ7.M61263Fl 2010
  [Fic]--dc22   2009013565

Summary: Davis Miller is a puny, little mouse at Mount Tabor High School. After years of being bullied, the sickly teen decides
to become a boxer. Then one day, he gets a chance to spar with his hero, Muhammad Ali — a bout that will change his life.

Printed in the United States of America

CONTENTS

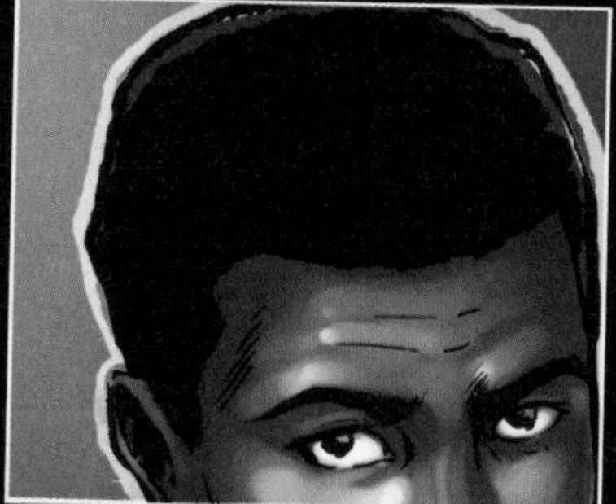

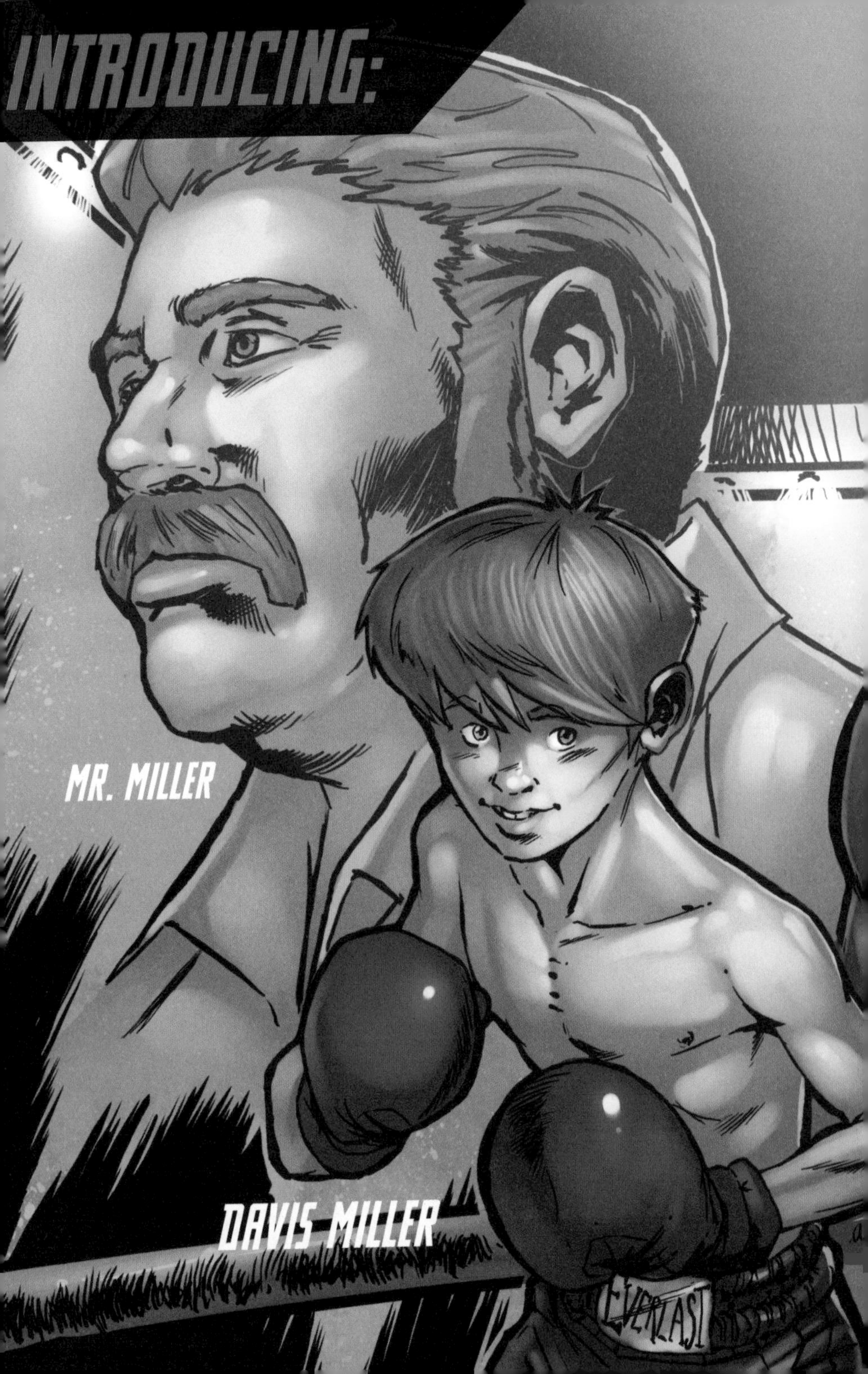
INTRODUCING:
MR. MILLER
DAVIS MILLER
EVERLAST

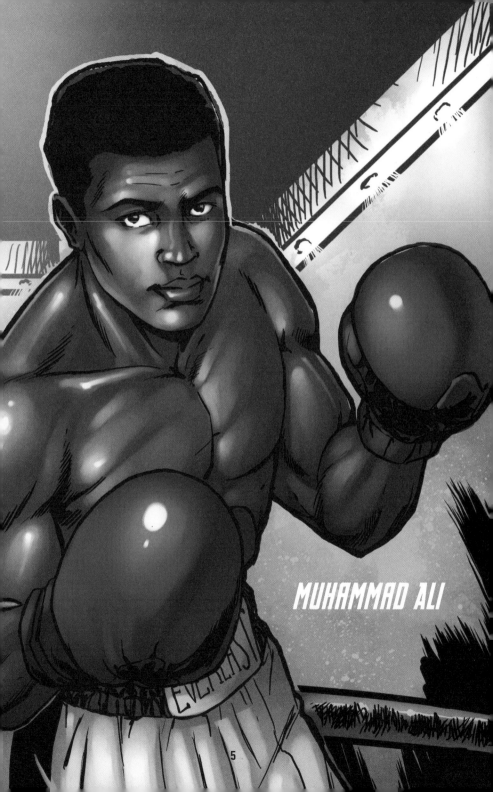

MUHAMMAD ALI

Mount Tabor High School, Winston-Salem, North Carolina. October, 1974.

My name is Mouse.

6

CHAPTER 1

BIG, WALLOPING SECRET

For years I've been smaller than everybody else my age. I'm 17 years old, 4-feet-9-inches tall, and I weigh 60 pounds. My family doctor, Dr. Glenn, says I'm never going to get much bigger.

My size is the reason guys at school call me Mouse. That, and the fact I have stand-up-high ears. I also have a small, twitchy mouth that sits way back behind my too-big nose.

The name my parents gave me isn't Mouse. It's Davis. But I almost never get called by my real name. When guys aren't calling me Mouse, they're doing other stuff to me. They punch me in the stomach, push me into girls' restrooms, or lock my skinny bones up in lockers.

Sometimes they drag me across the courtyard through the mud.

I don't want this stuff done to me.

But I'm not big enough or fast enough to do anything about it.

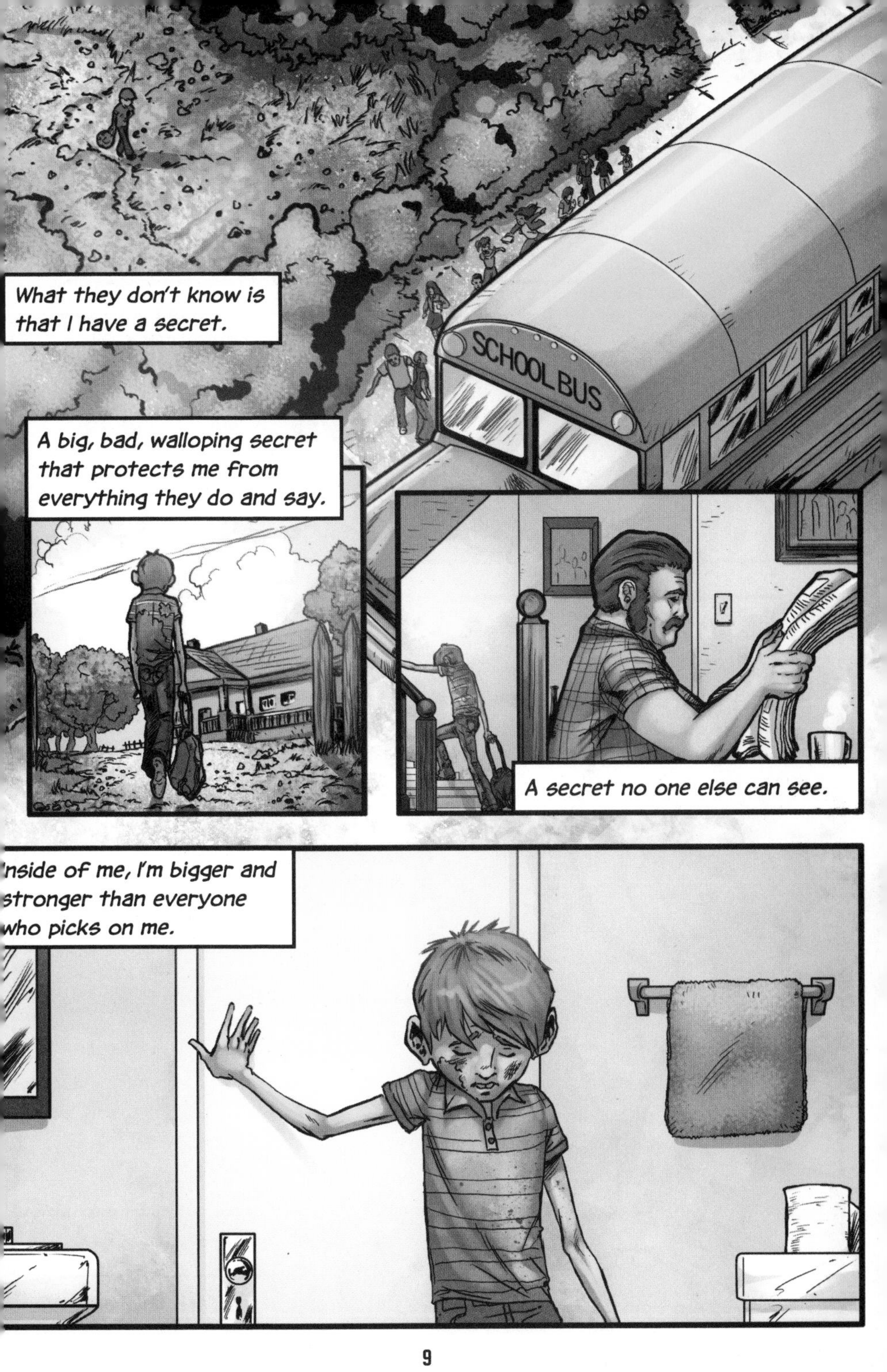
What they don't know is that I have a secret.
SCHOOL BUS
A big, bad, walloping secret that protects me from everything they do and say.
A secret no one else can see.
Inside of me, I'm bigger and stronger than everyone who picks on me.

Inside of me, I'm the biggest and strongest.

I'm the fastest and the greatest man in the world.

Inside of me . . .

. . . I'm Muhammad Ali.

Of course, I'm not really Muhammad Ali. He's the king of boxing and the most famous man in the world. I'm just a puny mouse at Mount Tabor High School.

But for months and months, I've been looking hard at my life. Today, I've made a decision. I'm going to become just like Ali — at least, as much like him as I can be, considering the tiny little me I'm forced to work with.

I first saw Ali in January 1964, six months after my mom died in a car accident. I was seven years old, and the sickliest kid in town. After the accident, I felt so awful that I shut myself off from the world.

That fall, my dad rushed me to the hospital a couple times. Doctors and nurses stuck long, fat needles in me. They pumped me full of fluids and fed me through tubes because I wouldn't eat or drink anything.

When I wasn't in the hospital, I spent almost every moment staring at the TV. I didn't feel like talking to anyone. I didn't even feel like getting up from the sofa.

Ali was anything but silent, and he wasn't just lying around. He was 21 years old, but he acted like a ridiculous, noisy kid. I remember lying on the sofa, staring at Daddy's little black-and-white television while Ali was being interviewed. He was training to challenge the fierce and ferocious titleholder, Sonny Liston, for the biggest prize in sports — boxing's heavyweight championship of the world. Ali was loud, impossibly confident, and glowing.

Liston was the most feared man in boxing. He had demolished everyone who faced him, usually in less than five rounds. Most boxing people thought there was no one who could take Liston's title from him.

The only person who was taking Ali's chances seriously was Ali himself. When I saw Ali that first time, his voice roared and crackled from the huge, live world outside through the TV's tiny, rattling speaker. "Liston's too ugly to be champ," the voice said. "The champ should be pretty like me. I'm young and handsome and fast and pretty and can't possibly be beat."

*   *   *

The next month, Muhammad Ali surprised everybody by knocking out Liston with ease.

For the next several years, he whipped every person who stood in front of him in the ring. No one before had ever boxed the way Ali did. Even though I didn't know anything about boxing, I knew I was witnessing something and someone brand new in the world. Ali was different from anyone who had come before.

Most fighters held their gloved fists close to their ears.

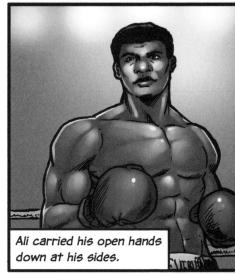

Ali carried his open hands down at his sides.

He danced quickly around the ring.

Ali looked beautifully in danger every moment he was boxing.

But the thing that kept him out of trouble . . .

He was the fastest man who ever fought.

Just two seconds into his fight with Brian London, Ali landed a mind-numbing series of seventeen blows. When he quit throwing punches, London crumpled to the canvas. Ali stepped back and thrusted his arms above his head in triumph.

Sitting in front of my father's television, I shook my head from side to side. How could a man as big as Ali snap out more than eight shockingly stiff punches in a single second? It didn't seem possible for anyone, much less a six-foot, three-inch-tall man who weighed 210 pounds.

The one time it appeared Ali would get beat wasn't in the boxing ring. It was when he went up against the United States government. In 1967, Ali refused to be drafted into the army. He explained that he was a Nation of Islam minister. He said that his religion and his personal beliefs didn't allow him to participate in the military.

Millions of people in America didn't like Ali's reason for not joining. They thought he was a coward and wanted him to go to jail. But in many places, he became a hero. Boxing authorities took away Ali's world championship and his license to box. He was convicted of draft evasion and sentenced to five years in prison. But, in June 1971, the Supreme Court declared that Ali had been wrongfully convicted.

Soon, Ali was back in the ring. His return cleared the way for what happened this past week. In Zaire, Africa, October 30, 1974, three months before his thirty-third birthday, "old man" Ali battled the young, undefeated, and seemingly invincible heavyweight king, George Foreman. Foreman's childhood hero had been Sonny Liston. Before the fight, almost everybody believed that Foreman, the hardest puncher ever in boxing, might actually kill Ali.

But Ali knocked out the supposedly unbeatable Foreman.

And the only person who wasn't surprised . . .

. . . was m

Suddenly, many people who had hated Ali now admired him.

I admire Ali because he had accomplished something so big.

And because he did things that no one thought were possible.

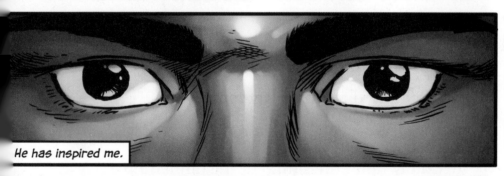

He has inspired me.

Maybe I can do something pretty good, too.

CHAPTER 2

MY FATHER

"You want to do what?" Daddy says when I tell him my plans.

"All I need is a year, Dad," I say.

"Dad?" he repeats. I usually call my father "Daddy." But I've been feeling pretty adult lately.

"I need to find out what I can do," I continue. "I need to see where I fit. I'm almost eighteen. I can't afford to waste any more time."

My father laughs. It's Sunday afternoon, and Daddy and I are sitting at the dinner table. We just finished gorging ourselves on a big roasted turkey, steamed carrots, and boiled potatoes. In the years since my mom died, Daddy's become a good cook.

"Son," my dad says, "I promised your mother that you'd get a college education. I would really hate to see you work some no-account second- or third-shift job most your life. I've had to do it, and I regret not getting a diploma. When you tell me that you don't want to go to college next year, I get worried. Life can get awful hard without a degree."

As Daddy talks, I remember stories my grandfather told me years ago. He told rich tales about his seven brothers and sisters, and the orphanages they lived in after their mother died. He told stories about brawling his way out of the Methodist Children's Home, and his years as a Merchant Marine. To me, Grandaddy's tales are as large as Aesop's fables. Maybe they feel even bigger, because they're about my own family. Stories of gold, or oranges, and cinnamon. Tales of storms, of shipwrecks, and of ghosts.

I remember some of my grandaddy's other stories, too. He told me tales of his son's baseball days. Daddy had been a talented player who'd been offered college scholarships. He told me stories about how Daddy chose to marry my mother instead of playing baseball.

Deeper than memory, I know what it was like for Daddy after they had gotten married. Daddy delivered newspapers every morning before going to work for ten hours in a cigarette factory. I remember that whenever Daddy got home and hugged me, he was always wearing sand-colored uniforms with black-and-white company patches on the breast pocket.

I know about better jobs Daddy was offered in Texas and Florida. He didn't take any of them. When I asked my grandaddy why, he explained, "You kids would have had to move."

or the first time in my life, I understand Daddy in way other than what he has provided for me.

addy doesn't have to say he supports my ecision not to go to college for a year.

I understand that he does.

As we talk, I feel memories loosen like last autumn's leaves in a spring rain . . .

. . . falling from the trees . . .

. . . and into the muddy water of the creek behind our house

CHAPTER 3

WORKING OUT

I buy a copy of the Ali biography, *Sting Like a Bee*. In the book, I discover that my birthday and Ali's are the same, January 17. I start working out the morning after our birthday — my eighteenth, and Ali's thirty-third. On Daddy's bathroom scale, I weigh 62 pounds. I get down on the floor and try to do my first-ever push-up.

When I've worn myself out on about five of these, I run twice around our backyard. My legs stiffen from lack of use. I finish my day with a few overhead presses with the 22-pound, baby-blue plastic weight set Daddy had gotten for me years ago. The next couple of mornings, I'm so sore that I can barely lift my arms over my head.

I stay with my workouts . . .

. . . through the winter . . .

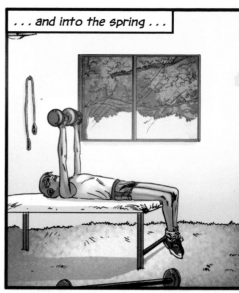

. . . and into the spring . . .

I ache from neck to big toes all day, every day.

But soon, I'm able to sprint around the yard.

I bound down the creek bank behind Daddy's house.

I splash through the water.

I continue toward Shaffner Park, creating my own five-mile path.

By then I'm pumping out push-ups in bunches. I do four sets of ten, twenty, then thirty, and now fifty. Eventually, I start to grind out more than five hundred a day.

In January, I started with five sit-ups each workout. By April, I'm at five hundred sit-ups. I do them six days a week, every week. I do a couple hundred crunches and leg raises, too.

I force myself to eat four giant meals every day. I also drink a gallon of milk and a couple blenders full of ice cream, bananas, and a powder for weight gain. I tip the bathroom scale to 95 pounds, then 105, 112, 121. And I start getting taller, too. In May, when I go to Dr. Glenn's office for my yearly physical, I measure in at a humongous five-foot-five.

I walk past the bathroom mirror in a pair of gym shorts. Out of the corner of my eye, I spot crisply defined torso muscles.

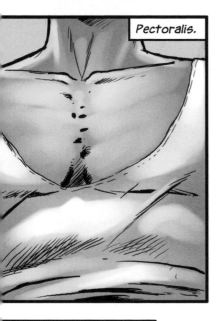

Pectoralis.

Abdominus.

Biceps.

For a second,
I wonder who
this person is
in the mirror.

Then I smile.

I start taking karate lessons because there's no boxing club in town. I buy a uniform and go to class religiously. I work as hard as I can. I kick at the walls. I punch the air, and other students, hundreds of times. I sweat and hurt for an hour and a half, three nights a week.

My favorite sparring partner is Eddie "Racecar" Ford. He's a fast, goofy, awkward guy who's only a couple inches taller than me. Racecar has pretty good kicks and okay hands. What makes him fun to spar against, though, is he's so awkward it's almost impossible to predict the ways he'll move. You can never tell what he'll throw at you next.

Daddy takes an old cotton laundry bag, fills it with rags, and ties it closed with a rope. Then he hangs it from a ceiling beam in the basement. I push my fists into that twenty-pound marshmallow a thousand times every day. I concentrate on speed and timing.

Dazzling, air-crackling speed.

POP!

WHAP!

Ali speed.

And I work to spring up on my toes, like Ali does.

FHOOSH!

I try to fly like Ali, bounding around the bag and to my left.

When I'm not working out, I devour every magazine about Ali I can find. I read every book and periodical about boxing and martial arts. As I continue to grow, the world seems to get bigger and bigger.

I travel from gym to gym and learn from anyone who will spar with me. I'll out-finesse and out-think opponents, but I don't like hurting anyone, or getting hurt. In fact, the idea of hurting another person makes me feel sick to my stomach.

I buy a full-length mirror, place it against a wall in the basement. I shadowbox every day in front of it. Pushing my wormy left arm out at the mirror, I try to imitate Ali's cobra-like jab. Like Ali, with every punch I throw, I blow the air from my lungs with a short, hot, "fuh" sound. I dance and punch and kick and talk at the mirror, trying to sound like Ali.

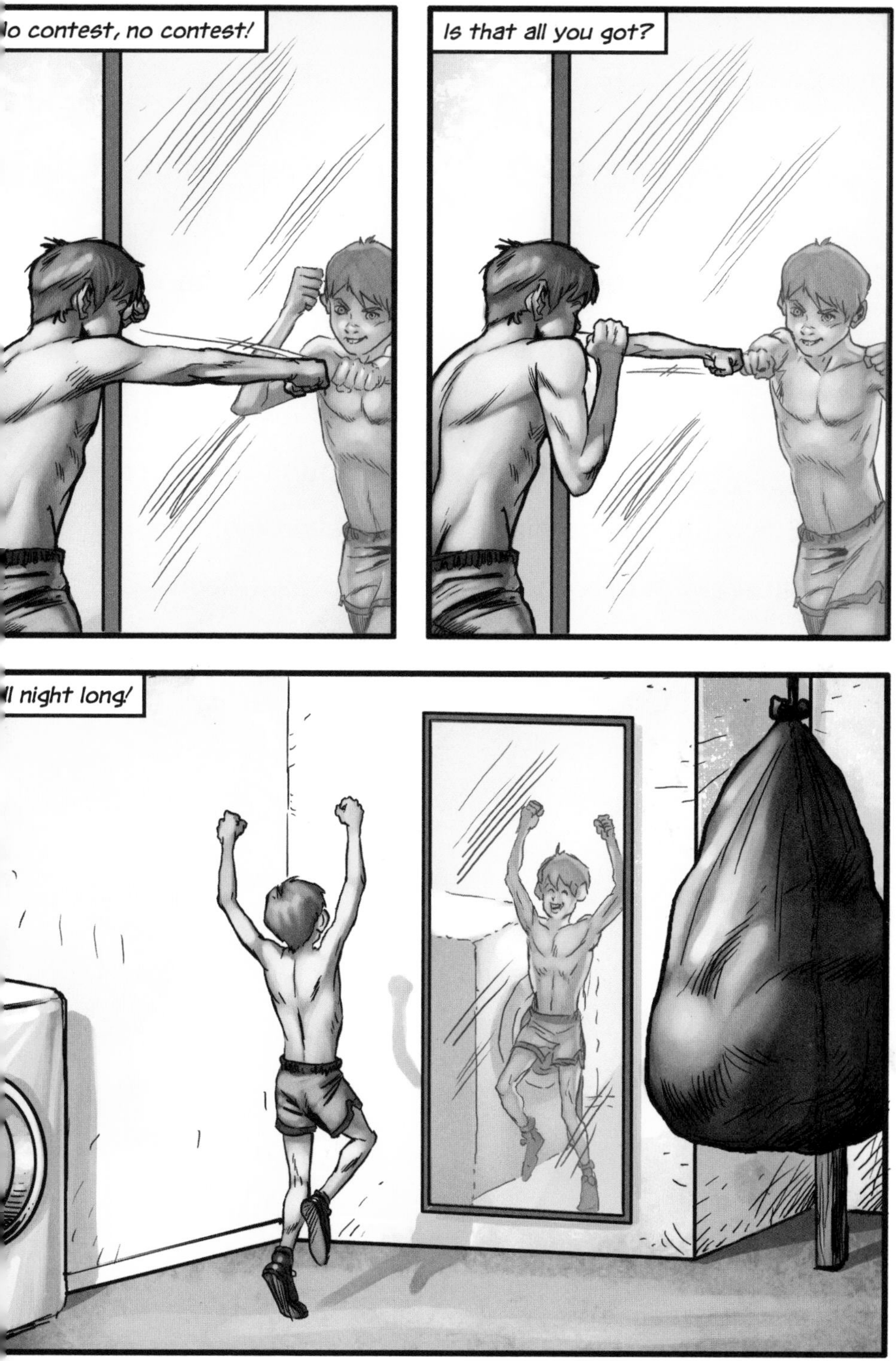
o contest, no contest!
Is that all you got?
l night long!

All of these phrases are Ali's own personal favorites. Whether it's hands, feet, head, or mouth, I focus on making everything seem effortless and look beautiful.

Popping the air with blows too fast to count, I imagine lightning running through my limbs. Eventually, I can zing four, six, even eight crisp punches per second. Within months, I begin to feel I might be close to ready for the next step in my big plans.

CHAPTER 4

TRAINING CAMP

After graduation ceremonies, the Mount Tabor guys all leave for Myrtle Beach to get some sun. Instead, I load my car with workout gear. I drive for 700 miles from Winston-Salem to Ali's training camp in Deer Lake, Pennsylvania. That's where he's training to defend his championship against Joe Bugner, the British titleholder.

Tugging on the red Everlast boxing trunks I bought for this occasion, I hear him through the dressing room walls. He's entertaining maybe fifty people who each paid one dollar to watch him train. "I'll prove to the whole world that I am not only the greatest boxer of all times," he says, "I am the greatest martial artist."

His voice is booming and musical. When he speaks, I feel it rumbling in my chest and belly. Listening to him through the walls makes me so nervous I have to work hard to stop my legs from trembling.

The old guy finding me a small pair of red leather gloves looks at me and starts to laugh. "Ali won't hurt a little boy like you," he whispers to me.

I've finally learned not to think of myself as little. The old guy is stooped, his face long, his eyes yellow with age. "Nah, he won't hurt you," he tells me again. "Not too bad, anyway."

He gives me the red gloves. Then, he wraps athletic tape around my hands, and he leaves the cabin. I pace back and forth, staring at the room. The rough bark of the logs that make up the walls makes me think of crocodiles lining up to eat me alive.

To escape the crocs, I walk out the back door.

Boulders have been placed around the cabin. A name is painted on each one.

Each name is one of the best and most famous boxers ever.

I walk back around the side of the cabin and climb the biggest boulder of all.

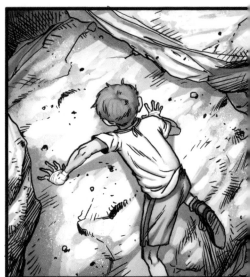

It's a tall hunk of hard rock named after the very first black heavyweight champion.

JACK JOHNSO

I stand on the rock, gloves hung around my neck. To calm myself and get my lungs started, I draw four deep, slow breaths. With each breath, I swear I feel oxygen rush all the way down to my toes and out past my fingers. I imagine the power of the earth flowing up from the boulder and into my body.

I'm ready, I tell myself. *I'm ready for this moment.*

Opening my eyes, I continue to breathe and to relax. I'm pretty sure what I've just told myself is true.

When I return to the gym, Ali is standing in the center of his ring. Splotches of dried blood dot the rough canvas.

I step through the ropes.

I stare up at him.

He comes into focus and everything else blurs.

CHAPTER 5

Ali points a gloved left fist at me. "This man's a great karate master," he says to the crowd.

I'm not a master of karate, or of anything else, but it makes me feel good to hear it. Staring straight at me, he opens his mouth. Then, in a voice directed not just to the people in the room but to the whole world, he shouts, "You must be a fool to get in the ring with me. When I'm through, you gonna think you been whupped by Bruce Lee." The crowd laughs. Though I feel embarrassed, I laugh with them.

"Are you scared?" he asks me. "How's it feel, knowin' you're standin' here with The Greatest of All Times?"

The bell rings, and suddenly I'm no longer nervous. My legs are strong and full of spring, and there's looseness in my movement. I notice men, women, and kids in the crowd. Almost every single person is smiling with anticipation.

He bounces from side to side in front of me. I feel each step he takes shoot into my feet and up my legs. I snap a long, uncertain front-kick up to his head. I figure it's the first kick he's ever had thrown at him, but he pulls away as easily as if he's been dodging feet his entire life.

He stops dancing and stands flat-footed in front of me. He studies my movements. Wow, what a gigantic man he is.

I try to sneak in a left jab. My arm is too short to reach him. His eyes are snappingly bright, his face is beaming and round and open. Sliding toward him, I launch a second jab. He waits until my punch is a half-inch from his nose.

hen he pulls his head traight back.

MOOOSH!

I punch nothing but air and dreams.

He drops his gloves to his sides and cranes his neck way out in my direction.

With a brisk wave of a glove, he motions for me to come in after him.

I skip inside his arms three half-steps. He's
so close I feel his breath on my shoulder. I dig
a roundkick into the soft area above his right
hipbone. I feel his flesh re-shape to that of
my shin. Now I see the opening I was hoping
to create. I fake a jab and rocket from my
crouch. I throw a spinning backfist-jab-left-hook
combination straight into the center of his jaw.
The punches feel so good I smile.

He opens his eyes wide in pretend disbelief.
For the next two seconds, I deserve his serious
attention. For two long seconds we are bound,
whirling in a galaxy of electricity. Each of us sees
nothing but the other man. For two week-long
seconds I am flying. Then he springs off of the
ropes and tags me with one quick jab.

I see the punch coming: a piece of shiny red
cinnamon candy exactly the size of a gloved fist. I
try to slip to the side and can't. It's *that* fast.

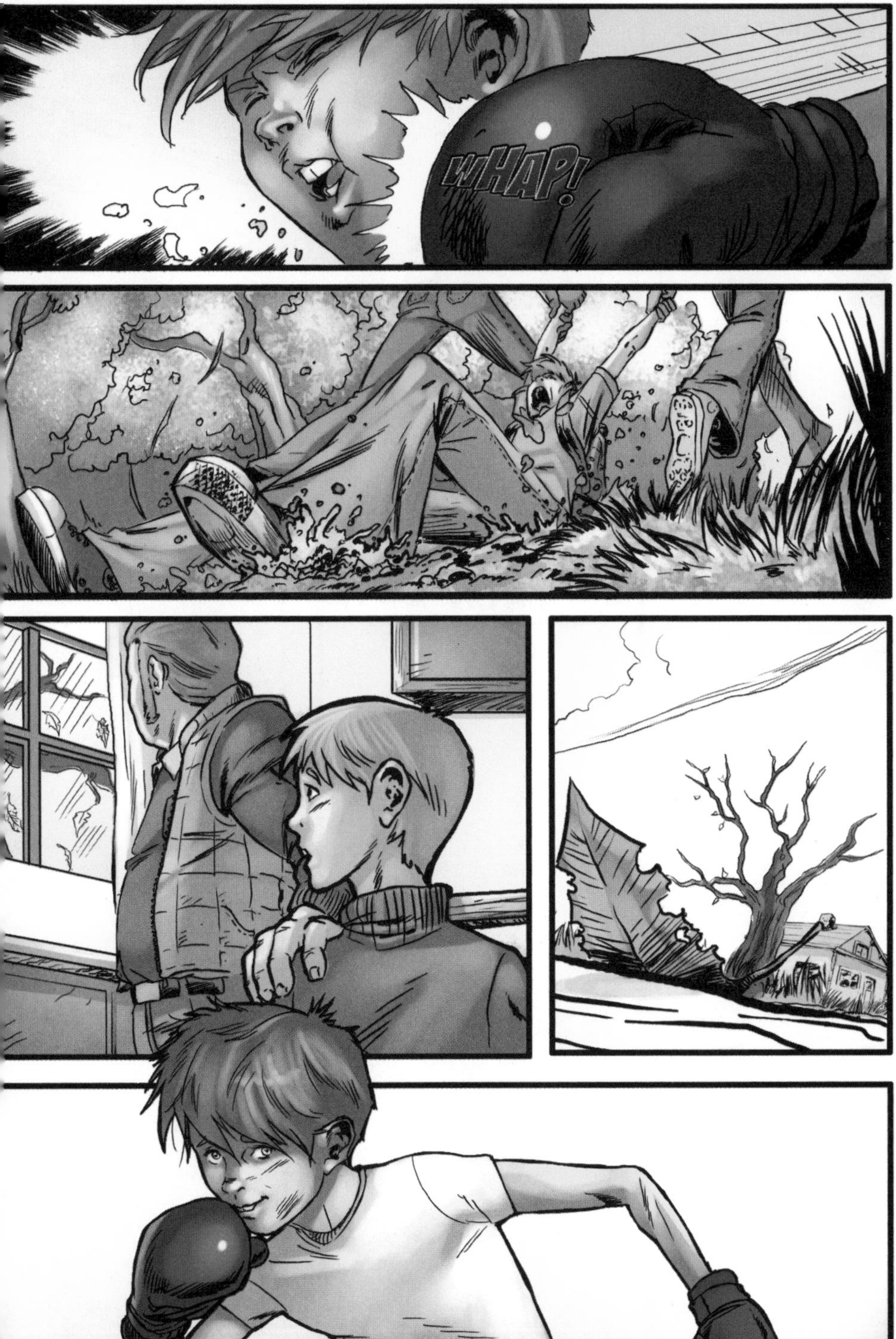
WHAP!

He knows I'm hurt, and he steps back.

He could easily knock me out with one more punch.

Instead, he slides his arms under mine.

It's over.

But I have now accomplished something I've never, yet always, believed I'd have the opportunity to do.

I have boxed with the world's greatest athlete, Muhammad Ali.

As we walk down the steps from the ring, my hero leans close to my ear and speaks to me. He talks in a way no man but my father has ever talked to me — softly, gently, almost purring.

"You're not as dumb as you look, kid," he says.

It's a line he must've used a thousand times. No matter how often I've heard him say it on TV, every time it makes me laugh.

"You're fast," he continues. "And you sure can hit for being so little."

He may as well have said he was thinking of adopting me.

I go dizzier than I think I've ever felt.

But I stay in control long enough to say the one thing I hope will impress him most:

With confidence I've learned from watching him countless times over all these years.

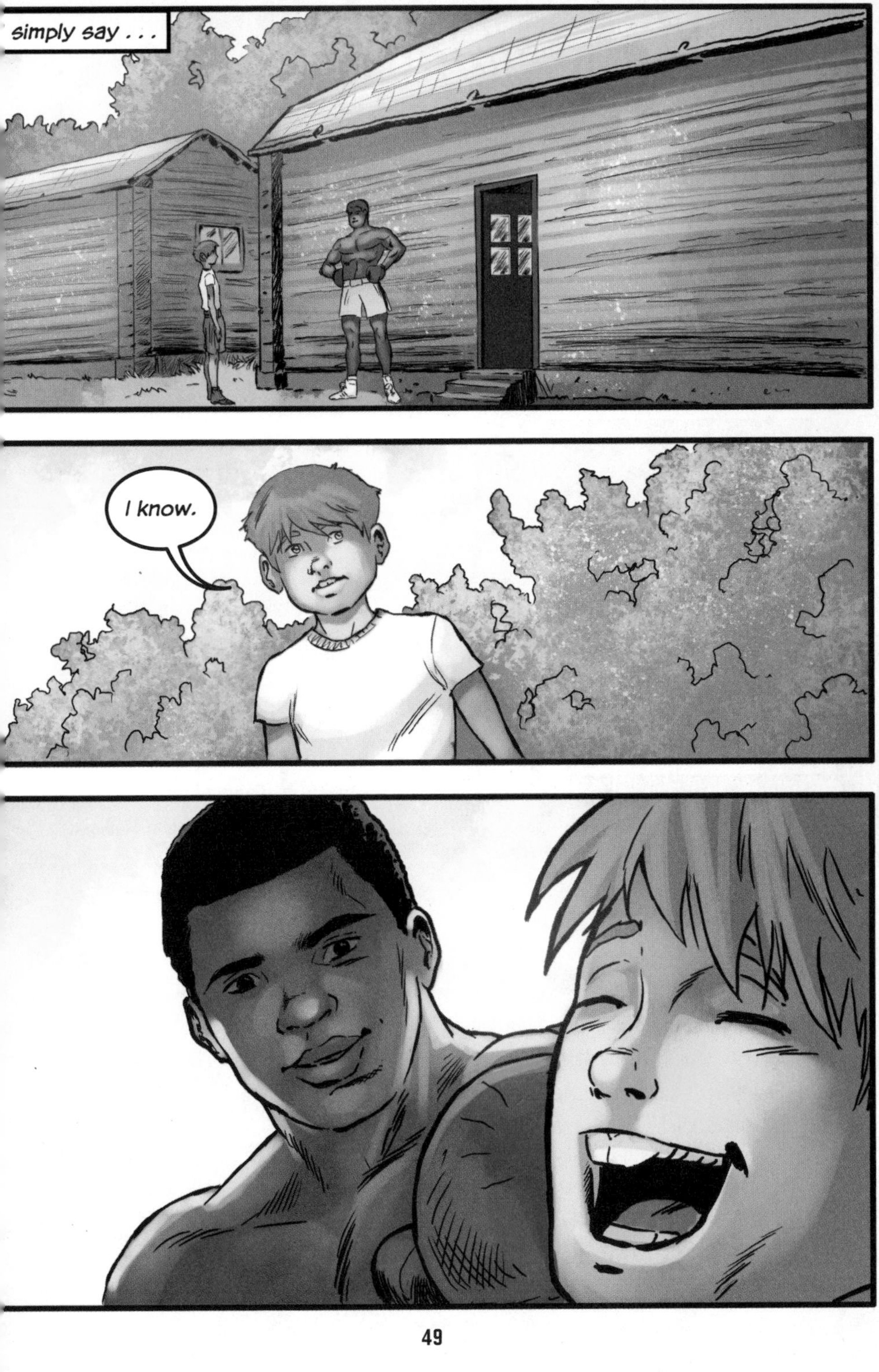
simply say . . .
I know.

MUHAMMAD ALI *TIME LINE*

1942: Ali is born January 17, as Cassius Clay Jr. in Louisville, Kentucky.

1960: Ali wins the light heavyweight gold medal in the 1960 Summer Olympics.

1964: February 25: Ali, a major underdog, knocks out Sonny Liston to become heavyweight champion. After winning, Ali speaks the famous line, "I shook up the world! I shook up the world!"

1964: On Friday, March 6, Cassius Clay takes the name Muhammad Ali.

1967: Ali is inducted into the military, but he refuses to serve, being a "conscientious objector" to the Vietnam War.

1971: The "Fight of the Century" with Joe Frazier takes place at Madison Square Garden. Ali suffers his first professional loss.

1974: October 30: "Rumble in the Jungle." Ali regains his title by defeating champion George Foreman. Before the fight, Ali said he would win because he would "float like a butterfly, sting like a bee."

1975: The "Thrilla in Manila": Ali defeats Joe Frazier. The fight lasts 14 rounds, and the temperature reaches 100 degrees.

1984: Ali is officially diagnosed with Parkinson's Syndrome. Since his diagnosis, Ali has said that he "regrets nothing."

1999: Ali is named Sportsman of the Century by *Sports Illustrated* magazine and the British Broadcasting Corporation. Suffering from Parkinson's, the 57-year-old Ali jokes that he may box once again. He receives a standing ovation from the crowd.

1996: Ali lights the Olympic torch at the opening ceremony in the 1996 Olympic Games in Atlanta.

2001: A biographical film entitled *Ali*, starring Will Smith, is released. The first thing Ali says about the role to Smith is: "You ain't pretty enough to play me."

2005: Ali receives the Presidential Medal of Freedom at a White House ceremony on November 9. The president pretends to throw a jab at Ali, who simply points his finger at his head and moves it in a circle around his ear, earning applause from the crowd.

1980   1990   2000   2010

ABOUT THE **AUTHOR**

Davis Miller is author of the book *The Tao of Muhammad Ali: A Fathers and Sons Memoir*, on which this story is based. He is also author of *The Tao of Bruce Lee: A Martial Arts Memoir* and *The Zen of Muhammad Ali and Other Obsessions*. Muhammad Ali was Davis's childhood hero. Davis has boxed with Ali on several occasions.

ABOUT THE **ILLUSTRATOR**

Andres Esparza was born in Monterrey, Nuevo Leon, Mexico on September 8, 1979. In the late 1980s, Andres's brother introduced him to the fantastic world of comic books, and he was hooked. Since then, Andres has studied graphic design at Universidad Metropolitana de Monterrey and has worked as an illustrator for a local newspaper called *El Norte*. He also contributes to a local comic book called *Melanie* and an alternative magazine call *PONX*.

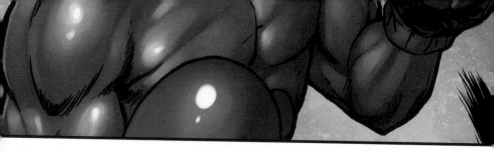

GLOSSARY

admired (ad-MIRED)—liked and respected someone

anticipation (an-tiss-uh-PAY-shuhn)—expectation, or looking forward to something

awkward (AWK-wurd)—uncoordinated or difficult

canvas (KAN-vuhss)—the cloth floor of a boxing ring that is stretched over a mat

demolished (di-MOL-ishd)—knocked down or destroyed something

fierce (FEERSS)—strong, dangerous, or intense

gorging (GORJ-ing)—stuffing yourself with food

religiously (ri-LIJ-uhss-lee)—in a committed and devoted manner

walloping (WOL-uhp-ing)—hard-hitting and powerful

DISCUSSION **QUESTIONS**

1. Mouse belives Muhammad Ali is the greatest athlete of all time. Who is your favorite athlete?

2. Who do you think was a more important role model to Mouse — Muhammad Ali, or Mouse's father? Why?

3. Half of this book is a graphic novel, and half is a traditional novel. Which style of storytelling do you like more?

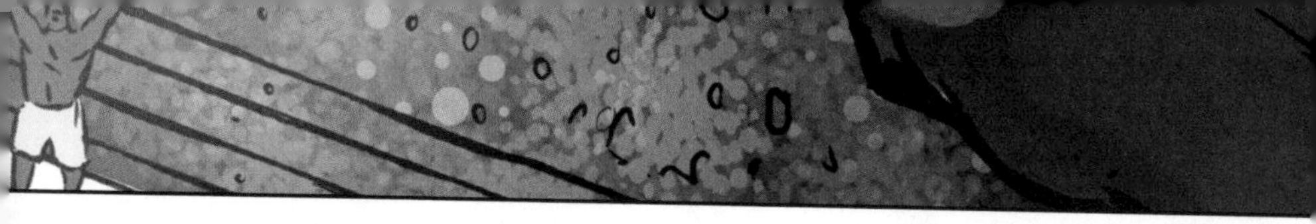

WRITING PROMPTS

1. Mouse achieves his dream when he gets to meet, and box, his role model, Muhammad Ali. What is your greatest dream? Do you think you'll ever achieve it? Write about your hopes and dreams.

2. Instead of going to college after he graduates high school, Mouse decides to train in martial arts and boxing for a year. What do you plan on doing after you graduate? Write about your plans for the future.

3. Mouse was always getting picked on by bullies. So he decided to work hard to become stronger and more confident in himself. What kinds of challenges have you overcome? How did you do it?

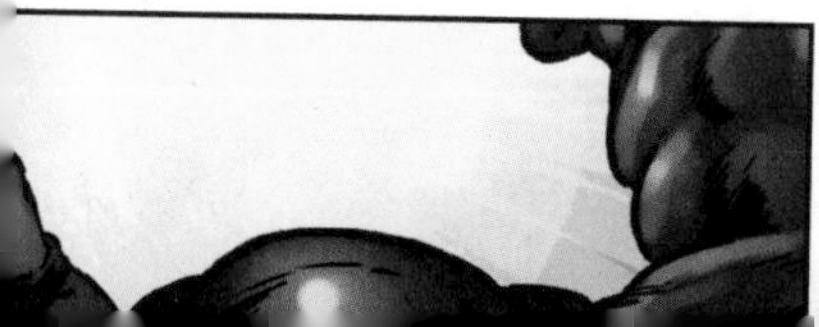

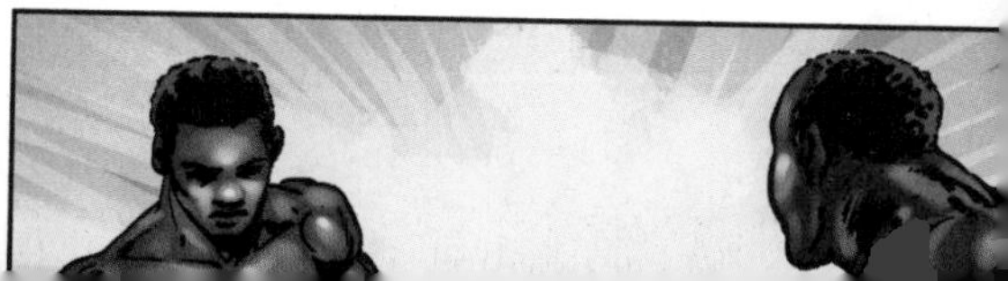

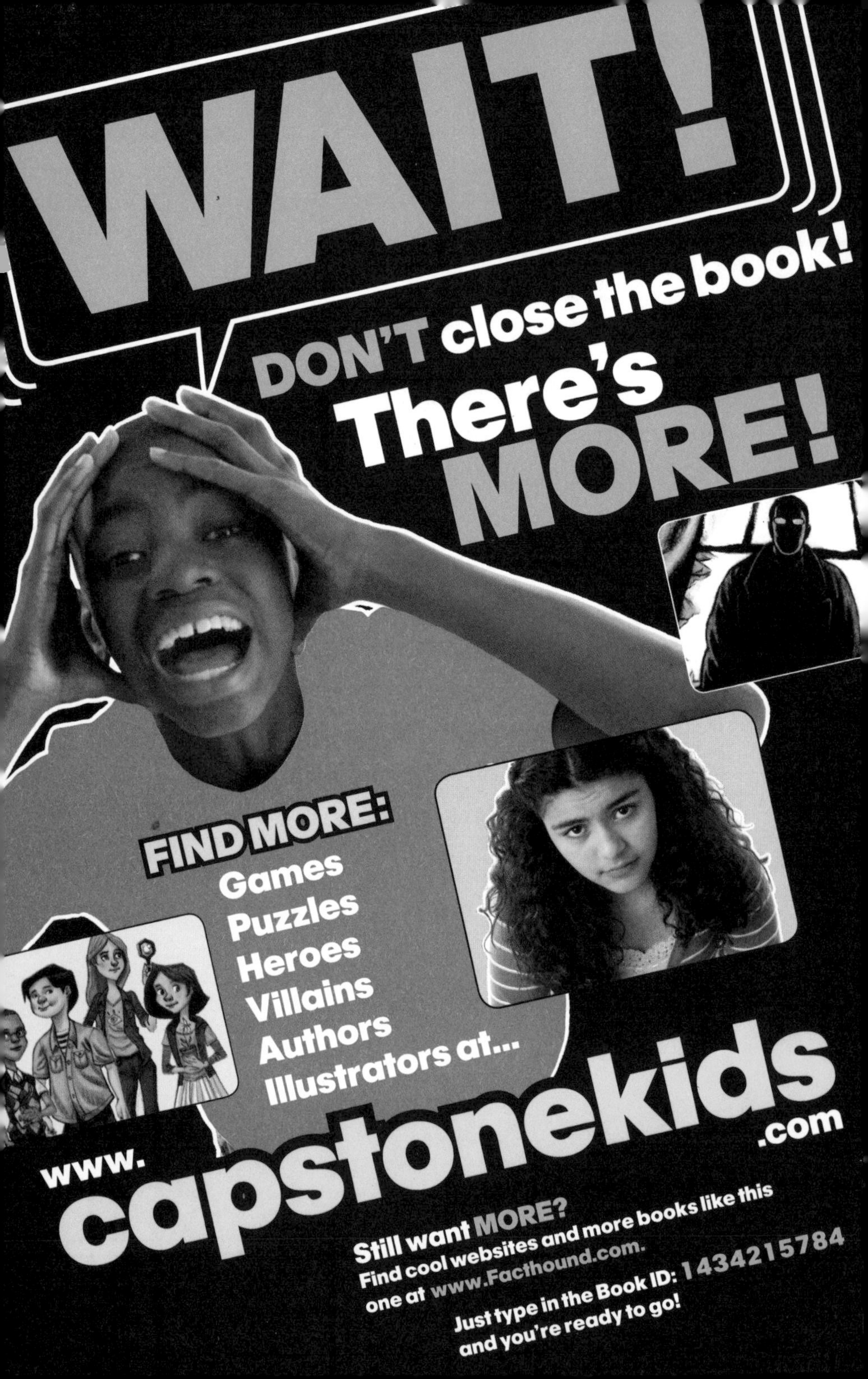
WAIT!
DON'T close the book!
There's MORE!
FIND MORE:
Games
Puzzles
Heroes
Villains
Authors
Illustrators at...
www.capstonekids.com
Still want MORE?
Find cool websites and more books like this one at www.Facthound.com.
Just type in the Book ID: 1434215784
and you're ready to go!